CHEERLEADING!

PAULINE FINBERG & PETER FILICHIA

SCHOLASTIC INC.
New York Toronto London Auckland Sydney

THE AUTHORS WOULD LIKE TO THANK:

From Hillcrest High School, Dallas, Texas
M. Alfonso, N. Carroccio, K. Clugston, J. McGuire,
E. Mahon, L. Pettigrew, R. Rand, K. Schulze,
R. Sinz, K. Smith, K. Williamson, and L. Gump.

From Miami Country Day School, Miami, Florida
P. Barry, A. Barwick, M. Ellenby, L. Feldman,
N. Harris, B. Horvath, A. Leeds, T. Mandel,
K. McKinnon, M. Rom, S. Stobs, N. Stolle, and
S. Widdekind.

From Arlington High School, Arlington, Massachusetts
R. Agostino, A. Burns, P. Grieco, P. McCormick,
L. Harding, D. Ciarcia, S. Marble, P. Neri, R. Neri,
C. O'Connor, L. Rodrigues, C. Stacchi, E. Stein,
and K. Terranova.

Special thanks to
M. Bower, J. Chamberlin, G. Cobb, V. D'Antona,
R. D'Antona, J. Filichia, G. Finberg, S. Finberg,
E. Ferrari, J. Harrison, L. Konner, B. Lowenstein,
B. Molloy, A. Reit, W. Wohllebe, D. Wolf, N. Davine.

Cover Photo by Gordan Kragich

ISBN 0-590-33417-4

24 23 22 21 20 19 18 17 16 15 14   2/0

CONTENTS

INTRODUCTION

So you want to be a cheerleader.

Well, you're in pretty good company. Carly Simon, Lily Tomlin, and Ann-Margret are all former cheerleaders. So are Dinah Shore, Raquel Welch, and Dyan Cannon.

The fact is, cheerleaders often go on to become other kinds of leaders, too. Many industrial magnates and presidents of major corporations once chanted cheers, performed with pom-pons, and rah-rahed their way through rousing routines. And as Johnny Carson has told many *Tonight Show* audiences, he's still upset at not having been selected a cheerleader in his high school.

For, despite criticism in the 1960s and 1970s, cheering is an all-American sport. Like jazz and musical comedy, it was born right here in the United States.

You may have assumed that cheering has been around since the year one, but it hasn't. Don't bother to look in Roman history books for information on the cheerleaders who rooted for the gladiators—you won't find anything. Cheering is less than a century old.

You are becoming a cheerleader at a good time in the sport's history. The era of branding cheerleaders as good-looking airheads is over. More and more people are realizing that cheering is a good sport in which kids can get involved, and one that requires time and effort. "Considering that kids are faced with negative options wherever they turn almost every day of their lives," says Carol, a former cheerleader, "cheering gives them an opportunity to get involved. They can shout encouraging words to their friends and peers. 'Hey!' you're telling those kids on the field, 'we know you're working, we know you want to win. We care, too.' There's something nice about that."

She's right. Cheering's a terrific pastime *and* a terrific amount of work. That's why this book was written: to help you enjoy the highs and deal with the lows.

Part One

Becoming a Cheerleader

The Ten Prerequisites for a Good Cheerleader

1. Do you have self-confidence? Cheering will develop your confidence, but you must have enough confidence in yourself to begin with. Otherwise, how are you going to get up in front of thousands of people at a game? For that matter, how are you going to perform in front of 60 or 70 other would-be cheerleaders and the judges at tryouts?

2. Are you good at making eye contact? It's one of the most important ingredients in a squad's success, but one of the biggest problems for most beginning cheerleaders.

3. Do you care enough about your school? If you think that it's a terrible place and not nearly as good as other schools you've heard about, you might not be able to cheer convincingly, no matter how hard you try.

But if you do care for your school, you'll come to appreciate it even more if you become a cheerleader. That's because you'll get to know the people who run the school: the superintendents and the principal. They'll see you in a positive light, as an upstanding member of the school community who'll bring glory to the alma mater. As you come to understand each of these people and his or her complicated job of keeping the school running, you'll fully believe what you're proclaiming on the field and in the arena.

4. Do you have a good voice? You don't have to be able to sing arias from Italian operas, but you shouldn't be too soft-spoken. Cheerleaders should be seen *and* heard.

5. How is your enunciation? If you have a tendency to say "comin' " instead of "coming," "jist" instead of "just," and "whoosh" instead of "wish," it's time to get to work at improving your diction.

6. Do you have at least a C average in all your subjects? Like most sports, cheering demands that you be academically competent. You must be if you're going to be on a time-consuming, energy-exhausting squad.

7. If you work after school, will your boss at work understand that you'll need a good deal of time off? Many bosses won't. It's best to have a job as a waiter or waitress. Doughnut shops and fast-food places are best because the hours are flexible there. You can work atrocious early Sunday-morning shifts in exchange for freedom on Saturday afternoons; you'll be able to find other kids who'll swap shifts with you in an emergency.

8. Are you physically fit? A good cheerleader needs to be. Of course, if you're not *quite* in top shape, you'll find that cheering will remedy that in a hurry.

9. Do you have average looks? That's

right — *average*. Don't assume that you must be dazzling. The old stereotype of phenom-enal-looking teenagers with perfect faces and bodies is very out-of-date. If you don't believe this, take a look at the squad of cheerleaders in your school. You may find a few knockouts, but there most likely will be some boys and girls who are average kids.

If you're heavy and have tried losing weight but are just one of those kids who is going to be big and beautiful no matter what, go ahead and try out for the squad. If you can do the motions, make the jumps, and — most importantly — show the correct spirit, few squads will turn you down. One important note, however: Avoid tight clothes. They'll make you look heavier than you are.

10. Last and most certainly *not* least, do you have the time?

You'll have eight to ten hours of practice each week. You'll devote all day Saturday to football games and many weeknights to bas-ketball and hockey games. You'll set up signs on fences before a game; you'll decorate the team's locker room before the athletes arrive.

You'll shop for crepe paper and poster board. Then you'll make dozens of posters. Magic Markers will soon lose their magic.

You'll mimeograph the cheers for the other kids in school to learn. You'll do hundreds of things.

But most importantly, you'll have to keep those hours open for practice. After all, the other cheerleaders aren't going to be able to make much of a pyramid if the bottom left cornerstone isn't at practice.

Remember, too, that cheerleaders practice more than many other athletes, because a cheerleader's season often includes football, basketball, *and* hockey seasons. Most athletes, however, play only one sport.

How did you do with the ten prerequisites? If you scored yes on at least six or if you're planning to make some changes, read on!

Seven Qualities that Will Give You an Edge

1. Being a gymnast. People who can do flips and cartwheels are always welcome on a squad.

2. Being a dancer. All those years of recitals and practice will be much appreciated by your cheerleading adviser.

3. Having a nice smile. Cheerleaders are supposed to flash those pearly whites with great frequency.

4. Being excitable by nature. You want the crowd to believe that you're really into the sport you're cheering for.

5. Being optimistic. After all, cheerleaders are supposed to assume that their team is going to win.

6. Having a little ham in you. There's nothing wrong with being a little hammy when you're a cheerleader. Don't forget — you are giving a performance. Besides, cheerleaders should be a little bigger than life. If they weren't, they'd just be spectators in the stands.

Make sure you don't overdo the acting, however.

7. Are you well-regarded by your classmates and the faculty? The kids and teachers must respect you to accept you as a school leader.

If you have at least four of these qualities, you should definitely try out. You've got an excellent chance!

CHAPTER 2

Trying Out

Sometime between February and April, cheerleading tryouts will be held in your school. If you're planning to attend, start doing some homework before tryouts are even announced.

First, attend both a varsity and a junior varsity game at which the cheerleaders are performing. Watch them! What are they doing? Can you do that? Still want to?

Good!

Next, decide whether or not you want to try out for the varsity or junior varsity squad.

Your status as either a freshman, sophomore, junior, or senior could dictate which squad you'll be eligible for. Traditionally, junior varsity squads consist of ninth and tenth graders. Some junior varsity squads, however, have eleventh graders on the team, because the varsity squads in those schools are only seniors.

On the other hand, if you go to a school that has no restrictions on varsity or junior varsity, do what's logical. If you're one of the younger members of the school, try the junior varsity first. If you make it, you'll have a year of discovering what cheerleading life is like. And if you like that life, then you can try out for the varsity squad next year.

But if you're one of the older members of the school, and you hadn't given cheering a thought until this year, you still might as well try out for the varsity first. The junior varsity will be there as a backup.

At home, practice smiling in front of a mirror. You may find that you're not smiling as dazzlingly as you thought. *It can't be,* you'll think to yourself when you see your lackluster reflection. But mirrors don't lie.

Wherever you go, practice your eye contact. *Oh, great,* you say, *I hate looking people in the eye.*

That was yesterday. Today, you've changed. Today you realize that the fans in the stands are just people, and they take their cue from you.

Wear the school colors to tryouts. The judges won't have to wonder how you look in red and gray if you're wearing precisely that. Pick clothes that are comfortable, pressed, and clean. Most importantly, wear clothes that look good on you.

Use this trick employed by Broadway and Hollywood actors: If you're called back to try out on another day, wear the exact same clothes you wore the first time. The judges can then recognize and remember you at once.

A note to girls: Don't wear too much makeup. Wear only what you usually do. Now isn't the time to experiment with makeup.

In short, when going to tryouts, look as if you want to be a cheerleader. Wear matching clothes, have your hair neat, shine your shoes, and do everything else so that people will say, "Hey, doesn't that kid look like a cheerleader?"

On your way to tryouts, before you actually step into the gym, practice smiling and making eye contact with everyone you see. That should put you in the mood!

At tryouts, you'll be provided with cheers from the adviser. You'll be taught one cheer with all the motions. Then you'll receive one cheer in which you'll have to create the motions. Gymnasts, if you have a super gymnastics routine, now's the time to do it.

Don't think of this as showing off. Remember, you are competing with other people. Use all your skills to score a few extra points.

In contrast to that old line about empty barrels making the most noise, you'll find that the loudest contenders for the cheerleading throne often get accepted, simply because they call more attention to themselves.

Don't be afraid of the cheerleading advisers. They're usually an understanding lot. Since they work very closely with a small number of students, often for a few years in a row, they've developed patience into an art form. They realize that Rome wasn't built in even a few days, so they're willing to bend over backward to give you a chance to make the squad. Quite often, if they see the smallest glimmer of potential, they take a chance and hope that you'll develop that potential later.

Cheerleading advisers also realize and remember what it's like to be a teenager. Little illnesses, big headaches, romantic problems, and battles with parents are all part of a cheer-leading adviser's hectic life, because they're part of a cheerleader's life.

Don't be afraid of the current cheerleaders who are judging you, but be aware that they will cast a very influential vote on whether or not you make the squad. These kids have seen it all in their cheerleading experiences, so don't blame them for being a little picky about your weaknesses. They know what it takes to be a cheerleader, and they want to make certain that the people who follow in their footsteps are capable of doing the job.

The judges are looking for someone with a good smile, someone who looks as if he or she is enjoying cheerleading. Therefore, you should show the judges a smile at *all* times. Even if you make a mistake, smile. You can always ask to start over again.

Sometimes the judges are teachers from your own school. This may pose a problem, because they come to tryouts with preconceived notions about you. Before you even step out to cheer, a judge could have already made a decision about you.

If you think that a judge is viewing you in a negative light, it's your job to change his or her mind by smiling and showing enthusiasm. If you're effective enough, you just might make that judge look at you differently.

Finally, it all comes down to how much you want it.

Some kids have been known to take speech courses so that they could improve their enunciation. Others took gymnastics so that they could improve their bodies. One kid even slept in the "herky" position (a famous cheerleading jump) so that she would do it correctly at tryouts. As it turned out, she was chosen over a kid who practiced only at the tryouts.

Prepare yourself for rejection, just in case.

Unfortunately, there just aren't enough jobs for all the people in the world. This even extends to a cheering squad.

We hate to dust off the old cliché, but if at first you don't succeed, try, try again. But don't assume that the judges and advisers are crazy, that you're much better than that stupid tall kid who made it, and that anyone who doubts this can just ask. Instead, ask the judges and the advisers — *pleasantly* — what you need to do to improve.

And listen to their advice. If two people agree that you're doing something wrong, they're probably right. You might as well just go ahead and correct it.

If you're rejected again and feel there is no way that you'll ever be accepted, look into other clubs and organizations. Needless to say, rejected cheerleaders (just like *accepted* cheerleaders) often go on to be class presidents, yearbook editors, and drama club stars. Keep telling yourself that Johnny Carson is a rejected cheerleader, too, and it hasn't hurt *his* career one bit!

BASIC ARM MOTIONS

Vertical down

Horizontal

Daggers

Low "V"

Diagonal

Punch

Hands on hips

Vertical up

High "V"

11

VARIATIONS
Daggers

BASIC HAND MOTIONS

Pail

Blade

Spider hand

Candlestick

Part Two

Being a
Cheerleader

CHAPTER 3

The Cheerleader as High School Student

If you made the squad, welcome to the world of cheerleading!

Now that your welcome is out of the way, let's correct some myths.

Cheerleading won't automatically make you popular.

Many new cheerleaders assume that they now hold the key to the school — if not the city. The plain fact, however, is that cheerleading often makes you *un*popular.

For one thing, some kids are jealous of cheerleaders. After all, it's an honor to be chosen for *any* selective organization, and kids who aren't accepted into clubs often rail against those who are.

You may also become unpopular with those kids who tried out for the cheering squad but didn't make it. Obviously, some of them are going to think that they should have been chosen instead of you.

The rest of the school may not welcome you with open arms, either. Sure, you'll be the envy of some, but there are many sports haters who believe that fighting for a funny-shaped ball for an hour is stupid. Needless to say, they think even less of the people who want to cheer and encourage these players. To them, you're guilty by association.

Football fanatics and basketball buffs may not take you seriously, either. To them, the on-field play is the thing; you're just window dressing, noisemakers, and jumpers.

"Once I got into cheerleading," says Mo, "I realized that it didn't do as much for my popularity as I thought it would. Kids still thought of me as Mo, not Mo the Cheerleader. And I guess," she says with a grin, "that that's the way it should be."

Some people will say, "Oh, that kid's a cheerleader? Must be all social and no smarts. Must take easy courses."

Why this happens isn't easily understood. After all, there's no rule that says you can't be more than one thing. But you're not going to be able to change people's minds by simply telling them, "Hey, I'm awfully social, but I'm awfully smart, too." What you must do, of course, is *show* them how smart you are. Act intelligently. Make the honor roll. Make the National Honor Society. Try to get into a good college.

In a way, a cheerleader *must* be smarter than the average high school student so that people won't think otherwise. "Why do I have to do anything for these people?" you might (rightfully) ask. "Who cares what they think? They're just jealous."

While your instincts may be correct, you must keep in mind that some of these adversaries will be people you just may have to deal with. So do your best.

For better or worse, then, cheering is its own reward. It doesn't make you popular, but it does put you in the limelight. For this reason, you'll have to behave yourself.

Don't get suspended for anything, certainly not for something stupid. If there's a cheerleading practice after school, and you've left your uniform at home, don't just leave school and hope that nobody sees you. Get permission via phone from your parent or guardian to go home. If that's impossible, then just stay and accept your mistake and bear the responsibility for it.

If you need a note from the coach in order to be out in the hallways decorating, get the note. Don't figure that they'll see you in your uniform and know what you're doing. Rules are made to be followed, and if you don't go along with them, especially while wearing your uniform, trouble for you, the squad, and your adviser is sure to follow.

Yes, it's hard to play the rules, to get to class on time, even to *go* to class at times. Sometimes it's impossible to avoid fights in the cafeteria. But you'll have to do all this and more.

You may also find that some teachers will expect more from you now that you're a cheerleader.

Somewhere along the line, someone determined that cheerleaders behave perfectly at all times. Of course it's an impossibility, but some believe it, so watch out when you're less than "perfect."

Some teachers assume that because a cheerleader is a class leader, he or she should inspire the other kids in class. Other teachers go to cheerleading advisers and discuss the cheerleader's poor grades with them, often adding, "The kid is so interested in cheerleading that he's interested in nothing else." Make certain that you do your job in class so that your teachers won't have any real complaints.

Gym teachers are often critical of cheerleaders who don't perform physical miracles in class. They're not trying to be mean; they just think of cheerleaders as athletes and expect them to perform that way.

Finally, no matter what you've heard, most teachers will *not* allow cheerleaders out of class to perform cheering-related duties.

You may have been, up till now, only a casual observer of sports. Cheering is going to change all that. If you're going to be a good cheerleader, you're going to have to be involved in the game. The crowd needs to hear your heart in your cheers.

There are a few things you'll need to know in order to understand and enjoy a game. So start watching *Monday Night Football, Game of the Week, Wide World of Sports,* and any other sports programs on your local television stations. You'll learn by watching those passes fly through the air, and you'll realize what happens when the guys at the other end of the playing area catch them and what happens when they don't.

Listen to the announcers. They'll tell you what the rules and concepts are. Tune into a highlights show; then you'll know what the big plays look like.

Eventually, you'll know sports a lot better; inevitably you'll feel more a part of sports, which is exactly what you're trying to do.

You'll pick up a whole new vocabulary in the effort, which will help you in conversation with members of the team. They'll be glad to know that the people cheering for them really know what's going on — and care.

Finally, now that you're a cheerleader, you may run the risk of losing the friendship of other students.

You'll try not to let cheerleading interfere with your friendships. But it's a hard job.

You'll especially run into difficulty with your friends who tried out for the squad but didn't make it. "There were times," remembers Ellen, "when I wished that *I* hadn't made the squad, since none of my friends did. All I could do was try to encourage them to try out next year. It didn't work. They soon dropped me."

"I had no intention of dropping my other friends," recalls Betty, "but a cheerleader spends plenty of time in cheerleading-related activities. Fridays down at the center become Friday-night sleepovers. And sleepovers are limited to cheerleaders only."

It happens. You'll try to spare your other friends the talk about the upcoming game or the post-practice party. Eventually, the other kids will sense that you're holding back and perhaps remove themselves from your life, whether you want them to or not. Do the best you can in holding on to all your friendships, but don't hate yourself if you can't.

CHAPTER 4

Helpful Conditioning Hints

Gary Sharp, Greg Webb, and Jeff Webb are three cheerleaders who work with the Universal Cheerleaders Association. Together, they've developed a program they feel is advantageous to keeping cheerleaders in good health.

"Cheerleading has changed drastically in the last five years," Gary says. "There's much greater emphasis now on jumps, tumbling, partner stunts, and pyramids. Because good cheerleaders must now be good athletes, a good conditioning program should be an important consideration for all serious squads."

"Being in shape will help you perform better," notes Greg. "You'll avoid injuries, look better on the field and court, and you'll generally feel better, too."

"Don't forget nutrition," warns Jeff. "We recommend a balanced diet that emphasizes fresh fruit and vegetables, whole wheat bread and cereals, protein—items like lean meat, fish, and poultry—and dairy group foods like low-fat milk and cottage cheese. Try to avoid or limit the intake of foods with high concentrations of sugar, fats, or caffeine."

"And of course, don't smoke," adds Gary. "If you do, it'll definitely affect your endurance."

"Weight is a big problem for most cheerleaders," says Greg. "Cheerleaders who are overweight run a higher risk of injury, restrict their ability to increase their skill levels, and usually limit their effectiveness on the field because of a less-than-satisfactory appearance."

"On the other hand," says Jeff, "those who maintain an appropriate weight will help decrease the potential for injury, be capable of improving their skills, and will have more confidence in front of the squad.

"We recommend aerobic [oxygen-related] and isotonic [tension-related] exercises. Any exercise that puts a constant stress on your legs is good. Walking, jogging, or swimming are all excellent endurance exercises. We recommend that any aerobic exercise you select be done for about twenty minutes four or five times a week."

If you are already physically fit, and if you have your doctor's approval, the three men suggest that you gradually work up to the following program: at least 20 cheerleading jumps per day, two or three sets of approximately 20 sit-ups per day, two sets of "as many push-ups as you can" per day, plus squeezing a hard rubber ball for 30 seconds in the palm of each hand.

"But where you really have to be careful," cautions Gary, "is in your ankles. Tumbling, jumps, and dismounts from partner stunts and pyramids all put considerable stress on your ankles. This is where most cheerleading injuries occur. Special emphasis should be placed on increasing the strength and flexibility of the ankles."

Cheerleaders have found the following exercises to be the most beneficial in strengthening ankles:

Toe lifts — Move your foot up and down, ideally with a suitable weight attached to your toe. Repeat this ten times.

Ankle rotation — Move your foot in a circular motion, once to the right, once to the left. This can be done with a weight attached to your upper foot or toe. Repeat this ten times.

Marble pickup — Try to pick up a marble with your toes. Repeat this ten times. (If you don't have a marble use a towel instead.)

Heel raising — Put the ball of your foot on any raised object, then raise the heel of your foot so that it is even with the raised object. Repeat this ten times.

Achilles stretch — Stand about three feet from the wall. With both feet flat on the floor, move your body toward the wall and then back. Repeat this ten times.

Lateral stretch — Slowly walk 50 yards on the outside edges of your feet, then walk back on the insides of your feet. Do this twice.

Resistance against towel — Put a towel around one foot. Then, with someone holding the towel down, slowly straighten the foot out. Repeat ten times for each foot.

Gary, Greg, and Jeff all feel that these ex-

ercises will make you a much better cheerleader, but they also stress that there is one
type of exercise that is absolutely essential for
cheerleading.

To find out about it, read on!

Exercising

The best and easiest way for cheerleaders
to exercise?

S-T-R-E-T-C-H.

Long before you start cheerleading, long before you attend cheerleading tryouts, *stretch*.
It's a simple exercise that may seem too simple
to you, but there's no denying the fact that
stretching will allow your body to deal with
everything cheerleading will do to it.

As soon as you get to practice, start stretching. Don't advance to splits in the first few
minutes of exercising; stretch. Talk, joke,
stretch. And keep stretching for at least 20
minutes. You don't have to do to anything
more ambitious until then; you don't have to
prove to anyone that you're Superman or Wonder Woman.

Anywhere you are, stretching is the most
convenient exercise you can do. Your body is
all the equipment you need to stretch and
stretch and stretch. And need we add that it's
inexpensive?

At home, stretch while you're watching television. Twist and turn, twist and stretch. Don't
bounce. Don't try to go too fast; pace yourself.

Ernie, a New York body-builder, stretches
and then goes on to other calisthenics while
visiting his friends. He'll do sit-ups and push-

ups while keeping up his end of the conversation. "This may look a little weird," he confesses, "but my body is grateful for the exercise."

Yours will be, too. Once you're all stretched out, start your sit-ups and push-ups. Don't forget rope-jumping. Boys, those heavyweight boxers have been telling you this for years. Girls, you've jumped before, you can jump again. In case you've forgotten: *A*, my name is Alice, I come from Alabama . . .

One more note to girls: You may be afraid of exercising too much. Some female cheerleaders worry that they'll wind up with fifteen-inch arms or something. "That won't happen," says Ernie. "You'll get no real increase in size, but you will get a thirty percent increase in strength.

"Nor will you get legs that resemble redwood tree trunks," Ernie continues. "As it turns out, a woman's legs are virtually as strong as a man's to begin with. If men have a physical advantage at all, it's concentrated in the top parts of their bodies.

"Look," he insists, "half of exercise is mental discipline. Any woman can beat a man in a marathon if she puts her mind to it. So swim and jog and bicycle yourself into shape. And don't forget about aerobics to condition your cardiovascular system."

But first, don't forget to stretch.

Injuries

Ever hear of a suicide jump? It's a popular stunt in the cheerleader's repertoire.

It begins with a running leap, and it ends in a split. But you know that when people name things, they don't throw in the word suicide unless there's a good reason for it.

And so, all too often when a cheerleader does a suicide jump, the result is a sharp pain.

Usually, it's the hamstring, those three muscles at the back of the knee that sometimes overextend when they're overflexed. It's a very painful injury.

Still, many times the injured cheerleader will smile and think, *I can't let the squad down . . . the show must go on.*

No, it mustn't. Stop in midroutine. Even if you think it's not the hamstring, *stop*, and don't move. If you continue performing, you might aggravate the injury; what would have been three days with a bandage becomes six weeks on crutches.

Be very careful when you're doing routines that require partner stunts, pyramids, and high mounts.

Now that gymnastics are more popular than ever, partner stunts, pyramids, and high mounts have been appearing with greater frequency. Admittedly, this has disturbed some people. Some schools have banned some of these routines because cheerleaders have been injured in the process of rehearsing or performing.

If you're on the bottom of a pyramid, remain still at all times. True, it's hard when people are climbing all over you, but you must remain still for their safety.

If you're a lightweight who's destined for the top of the pyramid, learn not only to climb up quickly but also be able to jump down even more quickly in case someone below cries out in pain. Common sense should dictate how high your high mounts will be. Yes, the audience enjoys seeing you climb to the sky, but that doesn't mean you *have* to do it!

Luckily, injuries in cheerleading are pretty uncommon. The Universal Cheerleaders Association did a survey on cheerleading-related injuries. Of the 10,000 students they surveyed, less than two percent had had injuries. And, of the 100-odd who did, 40 percent of them had pulled muscles and sprained ankles.

See? Not too bad.

Just watch out for that hamstring.

CHAPTER 5

Practice Sessions

"I remember the very first day I showed up at cheering practice," recollects Don. " 'Okay,' I said to everyone, 'now what exactly are we supposed to be doing?'

"Everybody laughed, but then the cheerleading adviser said, 'Some of the best questions are the most simple ones.' "

Don's question *is* a good question. As rudimentary as it sounds, it's important for each and every member of the squad to know exactly what he or she is supposed to do.

This is not as easy as it sounds. Although 12 kids may be listening to one opinion, it's common for four or five interpretations to result from that one speech. So pay attention; practice sessions are difficult enough to begin with.

You'll have a hard time just getting started at practice sessions. One of the hardest points to remember is that cheering isn't just a social club. When the coach or captain wants to start practice, that's it: The time for fooling around is over. Don't try to get in an extra moment of hilarity, and don't try to influence others into clowning around with you Remember: You're not "all social, no smarts." You know you can't waste these precious practice moments. If you do, you'll wish you had them back when you're actually on the field in front of an audience.

So what do you do at practice sessions?

You'll do chants, and you'll do cheers. In case you don't know the difference between them, a *chant* is a short expression ("Hooray for Arlington!") designed to encourage the audience to chant along with you. A *cheer* is a chant with motions. It usually ends in a pyramid or mount.

One of the objects of cheerleading is to fit one motion to each word or phrase of the cheer. The motions should be sharp, the words should fit, and the cheer should be loud.

Being loud enough is very important, of course. It's almost as important as having clear enunciation.

In order to get the loudest sound from your vocal cords and not injure them in the process, learn to project your voice from your diaphragm. Let it start deep within you; allow it to rise from the bottom of your stomach. Then roar out those words. Don't just *say* it—*feel* it!

You'll go through a great deal of trial and error before you learn to project from your diaphragm. Keep trying! Once you've mastered this technique, you won't have to worry about yelling too much. On the other hand, if you don't learn this method, you'll continue to be afraid of using your voice too much, and your voice will sound hesitant.

Of course, despite all your practice, you're going to do a good deal of yelling from your throat, once you're at a game and things get exciting. It's hard to change the habits of a lifetime.

Once you've mastered yelling, get to work on your enunciation.

Problems in enunciation seem worse when an entire squad makes the same mistakes. If you don't believe this, step away from the line and listen to your 11 colleagues. You'll hear the mistakes.

Make certain that you don't start *over*-enunciating. Of course, you can exaggerate the words for practice, until everyone is shouting the cheers crisply. Then relax a little bit, striking a balance between slurring the words and sounding like an Army drill team.

It's a good idea to start practice sessions with cheers and chants that you've already mastered. Doing the tried-and-true routines get you going, so that you can eventually tackle some rigorous new material.

But even as you do the routines that you could do in your sleep, make certain that you don't *look* as if you're doing them in your sleep. Infuse a freshness into each word, each motion. Pretend there's an audience out there and be as special as you can with each movement and sound. Remember to stay in line, too, and keep those hands on your hips when they belong there.

Some cheerleaders have a problem determining the actual starting point of a routine. Yes, everyone's agreed that you'll begin as soon as the captain says, "Ready, okay!" But when the signal is given, only a few kids start, while more than a few kids pause. The pausers think that "Ready, okay!" means that they still have to wait a beat or two before the cheer *really* starts.

Try something new. If you've been using "Ready, okay!" scrap it entirely. If "1-2-3" has been your starter, abandon it at once. Directors and choreographers like to use "5-6-7-8" as a count, because it sounds so distinctive. So try "5-6-7-8" and then start *on very next beat*. A fresh start will help everyone.

Incidentally, a good person to do the signal is a cheerleader who's positioned in the back of the line. During a game, he or she will be somewhat hidden from the audience, who won't be able to see his or her lips move. Your cheer will seem to start sharply out of nowhere, and that effect is a rather nice one.

You've heard of how important first impressions are. That's why the beginning of each routine you do must be sensational—so the audience will be on your side from the first moment.

Similarly, you've probably heard the expression, "the big finish." Make sure that your routine ends as spectacularly as it began. Go into it with the same enthusiasm with which you took the field. Also remember to put a "button" at the end of the cheer. That's the final shout that's designed to let the audience know that they can applaud.

If you're a little shaky midway through the routine, it won't hurt you as much as if your beginning or end is shaky. Somehow, spectators always seem to concentrate more at the start and finish. So if you make a terrible mistake midway through the program, a smashing finish will help everyone to forget.

Knowing when to *stop* practicing a cheer is important, too. Even the most disciplined squads go stale on a routine they've practiced one time too many. Once that terminal boredom sets in, it's hard to breathe life back into the routine.

Stop rehearsing, then, when you've all agreed that you've peaked.

Here's a trend that's become more and more popular: Cheerleaders performing to a famous song.

When choosing a song on which to build a routine, remember that some popular songs don't stay popular all that long. Some cheering squads prefer choosing a song that's become a standard so that they can use it year after year. Other squads believe that a song should only be used for a season, anyway, so they pick even the most fleeting-of-fame hit. What's your choice?

If you record your song on both reel-to-reel and cassette tapes, give them to the school's sound technician. He'll be able to play your song during your performance.

One last song suggestion: You might consider going back a few years and digging up songs that were popular. Then you can work out chants and cheers "For the Class of 19—" and sing the first eight bars of songs that were popular during that graduation year. It's been one of the more successful new routines.

Don't make each routine too long. In a game,

anything more than a minute-and-a-half is a problem. The audience will become bored. As they say in the theater, always leave them wanting more.

Merits and Demerits

Some cheerleading advisers feel a need to have a merit and demerit system to keep their cheerleaders in line.

If your adviser believes in this practice, he or she will equip you with a set of rules. The list will probably include some or all of the following: You'll receive a merit for consistent excellence of attitude, behavior, promptness, or any outstanding work. Each merit negates one demerit.

That's a good thing, too, because there are many ways a cheerleader can amass demerits: lateness; not being in appropriate dress for practice; being rude to fellow cheerleaders or visiting cheerleaders; not turning in money for uniforms, camp, etc.; wearing bracelets, necklaces, or the like when they would be safety hazards; unexcused absence from classes; gum chewing during games; profanity; leaving the game without notifying sponsors or authorities; wearing a uniform outside cheerleading events.

Your adviser may not feel the need to demerit *all* the above-named or may even have a few others not listed here, but you should be aware that such a system exists in some schools, and that you should try to discover in advance what the system is.

What you'll also learn from practice is that

everything isn't always as exciting as it looks from the outside.

In other words, sometimes it's hard to get along with your fellow cheerleaders, especially after a long and tiring practice. What's worse, being with the same people day after day after day can get on your nerves. You're ready to pull each other's fingernails out.

There *will* be conflicts. "Aren't we practicing that cheer too much?" "Why do I have to be at the bottom of the pyramid? The kid on top weighs a ton."

Sit down and talk things over. Go into the discussion with the belief that you will be better people at the end that you were when you started. View each issue as an opportunity to clear the air and start again, not as a threat that will drive you apart forever.

It'll all work out if you're calm about it.

CHAPTER 6

Fifty Chants to Cheer Your Team

Below are some of the more popular cheers used today. While some of them may look plain on paper, keep in mind that "you've got to be there" to really understand their appeal. Try them out with your squad; after a few minutes of work, they'll come alive. Then, after a few hours of working with various motions and emphasizing different words, you'll start to see real possibilities.

1. Thunder, thunder, thunderation
   We are (*school's name*) delegation.
   When we fight with determination,
   We create a unique sensation!

2. Hey! Hey!
   What do you say?
   Take that ball the other way!

3. Force the opposition
   To relinquish their position
   On the ball—hey! hey!
   Take that ball our way!

4. We're gonna win,
   And if you wonder why
   It's because we are the team
   From (*school's name*) High!

5. Go, go —
   Get 'em, get 'em
   No, no —
   Don't let 'em
   Win—win tonight,
   Just try with all your might!

6. B-E-A-T
   Beat 'em!
   B-U-S-T
   Bust 'em!
   Beat 'em! Bust 'em!
   That's our custom!
   Come on (*school's name*),
   Readjust 'em!

7. Block block block block
   Block block block block
   Block block block block
   Block those points!

8. We're mighty rough,
   We're mighty tough,
   We're the mighty (*team's nickname*).
   Now have you had enough?

9. Do it, (*team's nickname*),
   Do it, do it!
   You don't have to prove it,
   But do it, do it!

10. We don't want a loss, boys/girls,
   And we don't want a tie.
   We just want a victory
   For (*school's name*) High.

11. I say go,
   You say fight.
   Go! Fight! Go! Fight!
   I say win,
   You say tonight.
   Win tonight! Win tonight!
   I say all,
   You say right.
   Go fight,
   And go win tonight!

12. A-C-T
   I-O-N
   A-C-T-I-O-N
   We want *action*!

13. Say, people
   In the stands,
   Say, people,
   Clap your hands!
   Say, now
   You're in the groove!
   Say, team —
   Let's really move!

14. Say, hey,
   Everything's cool
   'Cuz we got a
   Terrific school!

15. Boom boom boom boom boom boom *right*!
   Boom! Our team is dynamite!

16. We've got the ball
In case you didn't know,
Come on (*team's nickname*),
Well, let's go!

17. The team is in a huddle.
The captain bows his head.
He's got 'em all together
And this is what he said:
"You gotta F-I-G-H-T
With all your M-I-G-H-T
You gotta boost that score!
Come on, team —
More! More! More!"

18. Back your team
All around,
And you'll see
They're victory bound!

19. Look up!
Be bold!
(*team's nickname*) Power —
Take a hold!

20. When it comes to winning
We're second to none.
And you know that means that
We're Number One!

21. We're gonna win today!
We're going all the way!
For we're (*spell out school's name*)
Hey!

22. Salt makes you thirsty,
Pepper makes you sneeze.

And our (*sport*) team
Makes 'em buckle at the knees!

23. We've got the pep,
And we've got the steam!
Don't believe us?
Take a look
At our (*sport*) team!

24. We know that we
Are the B-E-S-T!
Better, you see,
Than all the R-E-S-T!

25. V-I-C-T-O-R-Y!
Vict'ry! Vict'ry!
That's our cry!

26. Where there's smoke,
There's fire.
Where there's fire
There's heat.
And where our team is
There's a team that can't be beat!

27. Look at the time!
Look at the score!
Come on, (*school's name*)
We want more!

28. Can you dig it?
Can you dig it?
We'll win so so so so big, it
Will be such a rout
That's why we shout shout shout!

29. Oooh-oooh!
Ahhh-ahhh!
Easy as 1-2-3,
We'll see an oooh-ahhh
Victory!

30. What's between a zero
And the number two?
Number One, Number One
(*School's name*), that's you!

31. Straight ahead and on the track,
We are holding nothing back!
Hey, hey, one more time,
Hey, hey, it's score time!

32. 1-2-3-4
Who you gonna be for?
(*School's name*)!
(*School's name*)!
And they're gonna go for more!

33. We
We don't
We don't mess
We don't mess around —
As other teams have found!

34. We don't need the glory
So no player is a ham.
But we always get the glory
'Cuz the team goes bam-bam-bam!

35. Show 'em who's boss,
Show 'em a loss,
Show 'em where we've been —
Show that team a win!

36. We've got the fever,
We've got the beat,
We're gonna give our fans
A fan-fan-tastic treat!

37. There's a chap
Who can scrap
Shun a trap
Find a gap
As we clap
At his rapid scrap!

38. First and goal!
There's a hole!
Watch him roll!
Bless my soul!

39. Third and five!
Watch them drive!
Watch them strive—
And survive!

40. Watch them spin!
Watch them grin!
Watch — it's in,
And we win!

41. Watch 'em twirl
And curl.
Watch 'em whirl
And unfurl,
And right before the sack!
Oh, how we love to watch a
Scramblin' quarterback!

42. Hey, other team —
Sure, you're lookin' mean,

But you haven't seen
That Big (*team colors*) Machine!

43. Other team —
Are you set
To learn a little
Alphabet?
A, you aren't able,
So *B*, we're gonna boo,
'Cuz *C*, we can
And *D*, we're gonna do!

44. Hey, hey!
We're bad!
We're not just another fad.
Watch us! Watch us!
Other team, we'll make you mad!

45. He's our man!
What a man!
He's a (*school name*) man!
Yeah (*first name of player*)
Yeah (*last name of player*)
Yeah, yeah (*first and last name of player*)!

46. Sock! Sock!
Sock it to 'em!
Block! Block!
Block right through 'em!

47. Super super super super
Super super super duper.
Your team knows we are
A team of super superstars!

48. We're Number One
Under the sun,

Son of a gun,
We're Number One!

49. Hey (*school's name*),
Good, good try!
Hey (*other school*),
Good, good-bye!

50. Get it
Get it
Get it on!
Get that other team
Gone gone gone!

CHAPTER 7

Advice for Girl Cheerleaders

There's an old sports superstition that says, "Don't be the cheerleader who leads the cheer for your new boyfriend on the team, or he will become your *old* boyfriend very quickly."

We don't know how this rumor got started. Probably once upon a time too many cheer-leader-player couples broke up over the course of the season, and the tradition began.

Actually, we believe that just as you won't have any problems if you walk under ladders or have black cats walk past you, you and your boyfriend won't be doomed to extinction if you cheer his name. But it does bring up a bigger question: Should you date a member of the team in the first place?

You've probably heard many adults say such things as, "Don't ever date anyone in the office where you work." So, as a policy, should you avoid getting romantically entangled with a boy for whom you're cheering?

Almost all the cheerleaders we talked to said yes. But some disagree.

"Live dangerously," said Eve. "Going with

someone on the team gets you even more involved. You become more emotional than before, because you know how much the game means to your boyfriend."

"Another way of looking at it," says Peggy, "is that if you have a boyfriend on the team, you might as well be cheering for him, since you'd be at the games, anyway."

"I'd suggest, though," says Doris, a cheering adviser at a West Coast school, "that if you go with a boy on the team and then want to break up with him, *please* do it after the season. If he sees you at every game, you'll throw off his concentration. That'll make you lose *your* concentration. Then guess what happens to the concentration of the team and the squad when they see you not concentrating.

"What I'd most advise girls," says Doris, "is not to become a cheerleader just to get closer to a boy on the team. There are *many* easier ways to get to know him."

Advice for Boy Cheerleaders

Michael was a key member of Ohio State University's cheerleading squad in 1981. It was a good year to be a member of the squad, since it won the National Cheerleading Competition that year.

"But I wasn't a cheerleader in high school," says Mike. "There weren't any boy cheerleaders at our high school [Lima, Ohio] then.

"But it's changed," he says brightly. "Today, it's a little easier to do something different.

44

And since our school started treating cheerleading as a sport, plenty of guys try out every year.

"A lot of the boys told me that they like the other activities associated with cheerleading, too — speaking at banquets, publicizing games. And I told them that it gets even better when you're a cheerleader in college. For one thing, you get to travel. We play schools in Michigan, Illinois, and plenty of other places. In a good year, when the team is a potential national champion, we get to go to California. And when the school's picking up the tab, you enjoy traveling even more!

"I've met a ton of people and collected at least two tons of business cards. I've made some valuable contacts, and, believe me, I intend to contact plenty of them once I graduate and start looking for a job.

"But the biggest advantage of cheering is learning to be comfortable around other people. I've had to speak impromptu, both one on one and to throngs of people. I used to have a tough time with public speaking before. Now I don't, thanks to cheering."

"I had a pretty tough time being a high school cheerleader," says Guy, who performed this task at a St. Louis high school before going off to Ole Miss. "My problems stemmed from being a tumbler on the mini-tramp. It wasn't long before I was accused of being a one-man show.

"There still are some built-in prejudices against male cheerleaders," Guy adds. "It's too bad because cheerleading is a great sport, a fun pastime, and a terrific way to meet people. But tell the boys that they won't always be as welcome as the girls who go out for the squad."

Boys who are considering cheerleading but feel a bit awkward about going out for a traditionally female sport should talk to Lawrence Herkimer, the founder of the Dallas-based National Cheerleaders Association.

"Before the Second World War," he reports, "cheering was a male sport. It was considered too rough for girls then. But times changed, and that's why we hold special 'guy-talk' sessions to help boys cope with the problems they'll run into while cheering."

Perhaps you can hold some guy-talk sessions at your school, too. Remember to include some quick rebuttals to some rude comments you might hear.

"Being a boy cheerleader is a pretty big responsibility," says Jimmy. "If I drop a girl, the crowd looks at me with daggers in their eyes. And sometimes — not always, but sometimes — the reason I dropped the girl was because she didn't execute a move properly. But do you think that the crowd ever even thinks of that?"

"The best thing about being a male cheerleader," says Guido, "is that I'm an athlete at a football game, and I don't have to wear a helmet. Everyone who comes to the game knows exactly who I am!"

NCA staff members teach boy cheerleaders to maintain "strict business relations" with the girls on the squad. The feeling is that the squad can be ruined by intersquad squabbles between boyfriend and girl friend.

"In a way, that doesn't seem fair," laments Val. "Girl cheerleaders are allowed to date the football players. But I guess that's because the

girl cheerleader and the boy footba[ll]
aren't on the same team, while girl a[nd]
cheerleaders are."

"It's okay," says Mickey. "I never had [a sis]ter. Now I feel as if I had nine of them[.]"

FOOT
MOTIONS

Part Three

A Cheerleader's Equipment

CHAPTER 8

Uniforms

Trouble is, many schools today have a policy where cheerleaders must pay for their uniforms. In an era when school budgets are slashed mercilessly, superintendents claim there is nothing they can do.

Unfortunately, it's a rare kid today who can plunk down hundreds of dollars for a uniform. After all, it's not a good clothes investment. The cheerleader will wear it for a year or two at most, and then will probably wind up donating it to the school.

But if that's the policy of the school, there's nothing much anyone can do about it. What you *should* do, however, is check with your adviser in advance and find out exactly what your financial responsibilities are as a cheerleader.

Some schools are able to provide you with a uniform. Nevertheless, don't expect that you'll get it brand-new.

"We've gone to our sewing machines and have taken our uniforms in and let them out dozens of times," says Virginia, an adviser at an East Coast school. "And the athletic director tells me we have one uniform that has to be thirty years old."

"I believe that in our school," says Vicki, "you were chosen to be a cheerleader if you fit one of the uniforms they already had."

A word about shoes. When choosing shoes, go for comfort first, not style; this is good advice to apply to all your shoe purchases. The shoes that are safest are the ones with the most support for your feet. That doesn't mean they should be heavy; in fact, you should choose lightweight shoes, so that they won't hurt your partner when you climb into a pyramid.

Pom-Pons

You'll find that pom-pons are harder to handle than you would have thought.

It's hard to get twelve kids to do the same thing at the same time. Do you go up? Do you go down? Do you move these things sideways? Whichever, it's important to get it right. An audience might miss a hand or arm going the wrong way, but it's sure to notice a brightly-colored pom-pon that's going left when it should be going right.

Still, most squads agree that the effect you get from using pom-pons correctly is well worth the trouble. Quite simply, they look great. And — once you've mastered them — they're fun to use.

At first, when only a few kids seem to be handling them well, there will be the temptation to have only those few do the routine, while the rest of the squad sits it out. That's really not the answer. Put six pinpoint-perfect pom-ponners out on the field, and the audience is going to wonder why the other six of you *aren't* doing it. They'll realize that it's because you *can't* do it.

But you can. Let's face it: We're not talking about performing intricate brain surgery; we're talking about concentrating enough so that your mind is solely on the routine. It can be done!

In fact, you'll find that by the time the football season ends, you'll probably have mastered every pom-pon move — which is a shame, since the football season is really the only good time for pom-pons.

That's because you've got so much space when you're on the sidelines of a football field. But when you're cheering in the stands at a basketball game or a hockey game, you'll find that pom-pons are a nuisance, if not a genuine hazard. They seem much more weighty and far more awkward if you're in a crowd with them. If the pom-pons shred at all in the arena at a hockey game, the crepe paper on the ice can endanger the team.

No doubt about it: If you're off to cheer in a crowded arena, leave the pom-pons home.

Megaphones

"Megaphones are awkward," reports April, a former cheerleader. "You're always lifting them up and putting them down again. Then they're always tipping over, since they're only made of cardboard."

"What bothers me about the cardboard," says Carl, "is that the audience assumes the megaphones are made of something else. And then a big wind blows across the field, and your megaphone blows away. The whole thing looks very stupid."

"You need them when you're outdoors," says Myrna. "Luckily, you don't need them in an arena where everyone can hear you, anyway."

The choice is yours. But the effect of 12 cones pointed high and perfectly in the air is a nice one to strive for.

"All you have to do is practice," says Betsy. "Treat it as an extension of your arm. So many cheerleaders look as if they've never held one of these things before in their lives. It's probably because they haven't."

Springboard Trampolines

"My favorite thing about cheering," reminisces Chuck, "was the springboard trampoline. At the end of most cheers, I'd bounce away on a mini-tramp, do a few flips, and have a great time."

"Chuck was a gymnast when we got him," says Midge, his former adviser. "He'd been working with trampolines since he was nine. So we spent hundreds of dollars and bought him a mini-tramp, and I think it was money well spent for the years we used it.

"But since Chuck's time," Midge continued, "we haven't had anyone with his talent. Many have tried, most have failed — and a few got hurt."

Is there a moral to this story? Don't buy a mini-tramp (they're up to $400 now) unless you've got the gymnast who can use it. Talk with your advisers—they can tell you if they expect future cheerleaders to use it once this year's squad has gone on. It's a very special skill.

Emblems

There is other equipment you can buy. Open a catalogue from one of the cheerleading supply houses, and you'll find a cornucopia of cheerleading paraphernalia. You can buy award ribbons, bumper stickers, caps, detachable bibs, emblems, and far more.

The emblems, by the way, are made from a yarn called chenille, so the emblems themselves have come to be known as "chenilles." They come in all colors and in nearly every shade.

Chenilles offer plenty of options. For example, say your name is Terry and you go to to Temple High School. You'd like to have Terry printed in the stem of your *T* chenille? Done! Want to add your year of graduation? No problem. It may cost a dollar or two extra, of couse, but it can be done.

Part Four

The Game

CHAPTER 9

Before You Cheer at a Game

During lunchtime on the Friday before a game, set up a table in the cafeteria and pass out mimeographed chants. Find out which students will definitely be attending the game and try to arrange for them to sit in strategic places in the stands. After these "para-cheerleaders" learn the chants, they'll be able to roar encouragement to the team when the players need it most.

Girl cheerleaders should prepare themselves for some comments when they wear their short-skirted uniforms. Boys from your own school and the opposing school often have too much to say.

You may be tempted to fire back with some comments of your own. Don't. Two wrongs still don't make a right. The best defense, which politicians, athletes, and entertainers have been using for years, is to ignore the comments. The more completely you ignore them, the less confident they'll be that their remarks hurt you at all. When you silently walk away, you take away their audience.

Lastly, right now, before you start hanging around the candy machines in school lobbies, make a vow that you won't gain needless weight.

Often when you're at a game, you'll find that there just aren't that many places for you to eat. Fast food places may be your only option, unless you count a bag of potato chips from a local grocery store.

Make an effort to avoid this food. Make time to go to a nice place to eat or bring a good, brown-bag snack from home.

One note: You may discover that you've been delegated to cheer for a girls' team. We haven't *yet* reached the point in history when girls' athletics get the publicity boys' teams do. But even if girls' athletics were to achieve the status of boys' athletics overnight, some cheerleaders would still balk.

But there should be cheerleaders for girls' teams. The girls work as hard, and they deserve recognition, too. When you think of it, you're needed more at these games.

Cheering at a Game

Remember when you played "Sticky" in your kindergarten production of *Snow White and the Ten Dwarfs*? Remember how scared you were that you might forget your lines or do the wrong thing?

Well, once again you have the opportunity to perform. Only this time you'll be displaying your talents once a week, maybe more, in front of hundreds or thousands of people.

Don't panic. Remember: *People take their*

cue from you. If you act as if you have no right to be on the field, then few will believe that you do. But if you act poised, enthusiastic, and show that you know what you're doing (and *love* what you're doing), then the crowd will be convinced that you belong. You've got the uniform, you've got the time and attention, and therefore you've got the power. Appreciate it! Cherish it! Use It!

"Besides," as Rose notes, "not everyone's watching you anyway. Lots of people do watch you, but most of them watch the game!"

So don't be nervous and don't stare at your feet while you mumble the words. Eye contact is important, remember? So's your smile.

Find a friendly face in the crowd — your father, your mother, your sister, your brother, *anyone* who knows how important this moment is to you. These people are going to broadcast your smile right back to you and will offer you loads of encouragement in the process. Also, they'll feel like part of the game and will want to attend future events where you'll be performing.

You may also have to face all those who competed for your position on the squad. Some of them might prefer to see you fail. Don't let them! Instead of showing hesitation or awkwardness, show that smile.

When choosing people with whom to make eye contact, make certain that you pick fans you can trust. Some people can become awfully mischievous where cheerleaders are concerned. They've been known to make funny faces or to start giggling. In a flash, you're distracted, and you start to wonder if you've done something wrong or if you've got a stain on your uniform the size of Lake Michigan. Then the cheerleader next to you starts to feel your hesitation and flubs a bit. Soon the entire squad is off.

The chain is as strong as its weakest link. That's why it's best to make eye contact with the people who like you and want you to succeed.

"What cheer should we do next?" is an oft-asked question once the game is in progress. Too often, cheering squads fall into confusion as the kid on the left suggests one cheer, while the kid on the right demands another.

The captain is the one who will decide on which cheer will be done next. Period.

It's important for you to listen to your captain and then pass the word along the line so that everyone knows exactly what will happen next. This may sound obvious, but all too often in the heat of a game, you'll find that some cheerleader will get a mental block and won't be able to remember what to perform. If you're the one who's blocked, you'll be glad that someone was there to fill you in.

A word to captains: You'll soon find that there are logical places in the game where you can use certain cheers. For example, as the kicker is running to kick the ball, "Go-go-go-go-go" builds tension. Similarly, if you're cheering at a hockey game, We want a goal! We want a goal! is ideal during those times when players start to break away. And in basketball games, it's a good idea to yell out the center's name when he's jumping to get the ball. As Susan says, "It's a rush to hear your own name shouted to a crowd."

Use cheers that will explain the referees' signals. For example, in a football game, if you yell "We want a score!" you might punctuate the word "score" with both arms going straight up in the air — the referee's signal for a score.

At football games, however, you'll find it hard to synchronize your cheers with the referees' signals, since you're looking at the crowd and have your back to the field. Still, it can be done.

There are other good cheers that fit the game situation: "Change that score around!" when your team's behind; "Take that puck the other way!" when your team's not in possession. And when the football team is going for the point(s)-after-touchdown, you might chant:

> "Will they go for one point
> Or will they go for two?
> Hang on! Let's see
> What they're gonna do!"

This is a good example of why it's important to know the game you're cheering. If you didn't even know that a football team has the option of going for one point or two, you wouldn't understand this cheer.

This brings us to a related point: Pay attention to the game! Don't yell "We want a touchdown!" when the other team has the ball. Yes, there could be a fumble, and your team could then score, but the knowledgeable fan in the stands will know that you gave that cheer because you had no idea what was going on.

Use cheers that the fans in the stands can identify with. For example, cheers referring to the "Itty-bitty freshmen, the silly-silly sophomores, the jolly-jolly juniors, and the mighty-

mighty seniors" work because you have each of those classes well represented in the stands.

Another cheer that's pretty surefire is one in which you encourage each graduating class to name itself. Start with the graduation year of ten years ago and then go all the way up to the year in which the current freshmen will graduate. The alumni in the stands will holler back when they hear their class announced.

Some schools prefer to do this cheer the other way around (starting with the most recent year and working its way back), but you're better off increasing the years. That way, the cheer will accelerate with yells instead of petering out with whimpers (after all, there'll be many more current classmates in the stands than old-timers).

Another good cheer is an echo cheer. Yell "Ardee, Ardee, Ardee, Oh," and encourage the fans to echo it back to you; follow it with "Rickety, Rackety, Rickety-Ro," and they'll understand that you want them to say "Rickety, Rackety, Rickety-Ro" right back to you. Even the dullest of fans will have no problem remembering his or her lines.

Of course, it's easier to make the crowd feel like part of the game if you cheerleaders are part of the crowd yourselves. This is true for hockey and basketball games, where you sit in the stands with the paying customers. But if you're bordering the football field, you have to yell *to* the crowd if you're to have any impact. You want to see the game, you want to keep tabs on what's happening so you can chant the appropriate cheers, but you have to spend most of your time facing the fans.

You can't keep your back to them and expect them to respond to you.

The orchestration of your cheers is important, too. The rule of thumb is that you should do three short chants for every long cheer.

But you'll find that the game itself will set your pace. In a slow, dull game, use longer chants, so that you can add the excitement that's missing. But if the game is a thrill-a-minute nail-biter, use short chants— sometimes, just a couple of "Go's!" will do—so that you won't detract from the drama on the field.

Your biggest moments will come in the first period of play. That's because no matter how unsuccessful or magnificent your team has been in the past, it's a brand-new ballgame. Anything can happen; there could be a major upset in the making. If there's one thing the first period symbolizes, it is *hope*.

It's in the final period that the blues can set in. If the team isn't doing well, don't chant cheers that predict or indicate victory.

Of course, when your team is way behind, you'll find it hard to cheer with the same zip and joy you had earlier in the game. You'll also be tempted to go through the motions and do little more than mouth the cheers. This is expecially true at an away game, where there may be precious few of your fans in the stands. Even the players on your team may look at you as if to say, "What are *you* doing here?"

It is always your job to cheer, no matter what the circumstances. Do it.

When your team is ahead, don't project a victory too early in the game. The famous baseball cliché, "the game isn't over till the final out," is relevant to football, basketball, and hockey, too. Besides, if you start too early, your proclamations of victory might anger and inspire the opponents into making a miracle comeback.

And even if your opponents stand no chance of winning, don't mock them. As every sports fan knows, last year's champion can have a mediocre year this season, while this year's first-place team could have been last year's last-place team. Fame, glory, and winning are very fleeting in the sports world. Rub salt in another team's wounds, and they'll be there just waiting for the day when your team does poorly. There's an excellent chance that that day will come.

Therefore, you should use a positive approach to encourage your team, but you mustn't use a negative approach with the other team.

When you're at a football game, you're playing to a "big house." You've got 5,000 square yards of scenery behind you. Now's the time for the tallest mounts, biggest stunts, and your widest-sweeping motions.

That also means you keep the smaller motions for the more intimate arenas of basketball and hockey.

Adjust your chants and cheers to the sport and to the season. This cheer works for basketball and for hockey:
  "Ready, set—
    Put it in that net."
  But it wouldn't make sense in football. So:
  "Ready, roll—

Put it past the goal."

It may not be great poetry, but it means something in football.

A quick review before the first period should keep the squad from making these mistakes. While you're at it, get key words, such as field, ice, court, ball, and puck, into your pregame review, too.

When your team gets a penalty, or when a call goes the wrong way, don't boo the referees. Don't even look as if you're questioning them — and never mind what you see athletes doing to referees these days.

Since the advent of the instant replay, we've learned that referees are right far, far more often than wrong. It makes sense. How close was the referee to the play, and how much farther away were the spectators? And who was watching more closely? Who's been trained to watch closely?

But it all comes back to that instant replay. Our forefathers booed referees because they didn't have video-recorders to prove them wrong. If they had had the equipment, they would have thought differently, just as we do now whenever we see the play again.

Besides, you probably know how bad booing sounds whenever fans in the stands start to boo your team. Some fans may even boo *you* for cheering such a woebegone team.

Ignore them. Admittedly, it's easier at a hockey or basketball game, where you can turn away from the fans and cheer the team on the ice or on the court. At a football game, however, you're looking directly at the hostile crowd.

In these situations, stand with your hands

on your hips, and look as if you'll wait all day for them to be quiet. You've been trained to make eye contact with your crowd, so staring them down should be easier for you than it is for them.

Some fans will get bored, while others will realize it's not your fault. Eventually, you'll be able to continue your routine and even have a bit more attention than you would have had.

Lastly, sometimes the fans boo because it's too quiet—which means that you're not cheering enough.

Even if the crowd doesn't boo, it will get tired if the game is dull, no matter how much smiling and cheering you do. It's your job to keep their boredom to a minimum.

When you sense that the crowd is listless, huddle and review all the cheers you've done that day. Which ones did the crowd like most? Try those again; they may work one more time.

This is good advice even in exciting games, for dramatic contests have their share of penalties, delays, and timeouts, too. Make sure you have enough "chee-er en-er-gee" to last the balance of the afternoon.

When Not to Chant or Cheer

There are certain game situations which demand total silence.

First and foremost, be *absolutely quiet* when a player is injured, whether the player is on your team or on the opposing team. If the injury is serious enough for him to be carried off the field, give him a rousing round of applause as he leaves.

In basketball, when a player is going for a

penalty shot or a follow shot, he needs to concentrate. Do not chant or cheer.

When a team is in a huddle, it has a hard time hearing the game specifics because the audience is boisterous enough. Do not complicate matters by cheering.

When a team is just about to get a touchdown, it may need the sound of silence to help its concentration. Instead of chanting or cheering at this pressure-packed time, be silent—and instead prepare your touchdown cheer, which will (hopefully) follow.

You must be silent while the National Anthem is played.

C H A P T E R 10

Cheerleading Etiquette

When you're at a game, you're bound to see some of your friends in the stands. You may be tempted to leave the squad for a second so that you can go over and talk with them.

Of course, you're gone much more than a second, but even if you were able to make it back in *one second*, you shouldn't leave the squad. That behavior gives the crowd the impression that you're not immersed in the game.

You'll also embarrass your co-cheerleaders when they must come to get you, bring you back to the line, and refresh your memory of what's happening.

In bad weather during football season, you may want to just pack up and go home, rather than stand and be soaked on the field.

That's your right—but check with your adviser before you leave. Perhaps he or she will give you other directives.

While you're cheering a football game, you may become tired, so you'll decide to sit on the ground during those moments when you're not cheering.

Don't. To the fans in the stand, you'll look sloppy and lazy.

A seated cheerleader looks disinterested. For better or worse, a cheerleader, along with the cop on the beat, cannot sit down on the job.

These situations aren't nearly as difficult as dealing with the other cheerleading squad from your opponent's school.

Remember that the only real difference between your cheerleading squad and theirs is a geographic one. If you happened to live in their town, you'd be on their squad.

You're probably very similar people, then, with similar goals and ideas. And yet, you're adversaries, and each of you knows that. No matter how valiantly the opposing team plays, no matter how much the other side deserves to win, each of you wants your own team to win no matter what.

So most of the experiences that you'll have with visiting squads will be perfunctory meetings in which you'll smile, say hello, be cordial, and avoid anything outrageous.

Most likely there will be a halftime ceremony during football games, when you'll cheer for them and they'll cheer for you. The home-team cheering squad does a hello cheer, which is returned by the other squad. The home-team cheerleaders escort the visiting cheerleaders onto the field. There, a "friendship circle" is formed, with each home cheerleader alternating with each visiting cheerleader, as all form a circle in the middle of the field.

There are several variations on this procedure, of course, but whatever your squad does or encounters, make certain that you don't cause any problems when dealing with the other squad—no matter how intense the rivalry is between your school and theirs.

And those rivalries can really matter. "One time," remembers Dolly, "we thought it'd be a nice idea to bring the visiting squad some cookies we'd made. I can't tell you how many times we heard kids from that squad say, 'Hey, what's *in* these cookies, anyway?' "

"My advice concerning cheerleading etiquette," says Mamie, "is to check with the team's coach before you do *anything*. If you ride on the same bus as the team, check with the coach to see if he wants any cheering done while the team's on its way to the game. It's very possible that he'll want his kids concentrating on the game, not on all the wonderful things the cheerleaders are saying about the players. Our coach believed that the cheerleaders pumped up the kids much too much, so that they believed they could win without even trying. As a result, they often lost."

Moral of that story? Save your on-bus cheering for the ride home. Once the game is over, everyone can relax. Or cry.

Whether you're celebrating the thrill of victory or soothing the agony of defeat, ideally (and this is tough), your cheers and reaction to the team should be the same. A passer-by should not be able to tell from your faces and voices if your team won or lost.

And when the team arrives home, roll out the red carpet for them—literally, because a bolt of red fabric isn't all that costly. Give them a welcome home that'll be the icing on the cake or balm for their wounds.

Just as a football team's performance often overshadows a cheerleading squad's efforts, a cheerleading squad's performance often overshadows the band and the majorettes at a game.

It's too bad. All three squads are at the game to provide support for the team. Still, a team seems to relate more to the cheerleaders, probably because the cheerleaders decorated their school and locker room and made posters, too, while the band "only" played for them, and the majorettes "only" marched for them.

So the team thanks the cheerleaders and forgets to thank the other two squads. Then the band and majorettes understandably get hurt.

So, when the players come up to you after a game and say, "Hey, thanks for doing such a great job," you can respond with "You're welcome. And wasn't the band great, too? And how about those majorettes?" Hopefully they'll get the message.

After all, you know what it's like to work hard and not be thanked, and you don't wish that on anyone.

CHAPTER 11

Cheering at Tournaments

If your team is having a winning season, life seems great. Parties (and plenty of them) are given by kids, parents, and boosters. Cake and pretzels abound; the soda flows freely.

Enjoy such seasons, for, unfortunately, they are not that common. The 28 National Football League teams are well aware that the odds are 28-to-1 that their team will win the Super Bowl.

So, if your team is lucky enough to be in the running for a state championship, the odds are even more overwhelming. Therefore, be prepared for your team to lose en route to the big trophy.

Still, there's another way of looking at this. You may have heard about this way in which people are tested on their outlook on life: Someone half-fills a regular water glass with water, and then asks, "Is the glass half-empty or half-full?" Supposedly, the optimists say that the glass is half-full while the pessimists say that it is half-empty.

The point of this story? Realize that if your team is good enough to qualify for the tournaments, that is quite an achievement in itself. And if they don't win all the marbles, you must still view their season as a great success.

Since every school seems to be able to put out *one* team that has a shot to win it all, you'll probably find yourself deeply immersed during "tourney time." It's certainly one of the best times to be a cheerleader.

The team's excitement, coupled with your excitement, proves to be infectious. The students in school become excited, too. Kids will come up to you and ask about the status of the star center's knee, while kids who weren't able to attend last night's game will flock to you first thing in the morning for the good or bad news.

Of course, for all this time, energy, and work, your team may still lose the tournament. But you'll find that some player on the team— maybe the youngest, perhaps the shyest—but at least one team member will come up to you and say, "Thanks. You kids really did a great job for us. I appreciate it."

"It's a moment like that," notes Cassie, "that makes it all worthwhile."

Unfortunately, there's a dark side to tournaments. If your team wins, your opponent's fans won't be too happy. That means you must be prepared for the possibility of some rough goings-on.

Some hostile fans have been known to terrorize the buses of victorious teams. They've thrown objects at windshields, burst in the back doors, and even tried to tip the vehicles over.

These are difficult situations from which to escape. Since cheerleaders are always identifiable (this is the one time the uniform works against you), you are an easy target.

Two wrongs don't make a right, so employ passive resistance. It may not sound like a good course to follow when your life seems to be threatened, but no one has yet thought of anything better. Yes, it's hard to smile and keep walking when fans are throwing crushed Coke cans at you, but it's better than fighting back. That might lead to some broken bones. And should you get involved in a fight with some fan in T-shirt and jeans, those watching will know which school you represent, but not necessarily know which school your tormentor hails from.

These are the times when you'll be especially glad that the police and cheerleaders are on good terms.

Dealing with a Losing Team

If the kids on the team are having a bad season, they may not appreciate you very much. They may even come to resent you.

In a crazy way, that even makes sense.

Think of it. You're on the sidelines telling the crowd that this team is the greatest, this team is going to win, there's no stopping these guys, and they're out on the field getting shellacked 73–0 in the second quarter. As they hobble (or are carried) off the field, they hear your optimism. They look at you and glare, "What are you, crazy?"

Okay, you think, it's not *our* fault that you kids can't even make it close. And you're

right—it's not. But the[...]
rassed that they've let yo[...]
want to be around kids w[...]
crowd that they were going[...]
like to talk to them, and th[...]
the time to thank them.

Soon you'll feel like putti[...]
in their locker room. And n[...]
you, if you've been knocking y[...]
not being appreciated. As Paula said, "I wasn't
this team's slave, or its genie. I was a cheerleader. I tried being nice—we all tried being
nice—but these kids didn't care, no matter
what we did. We tried to find cheers that said
nothing about winning, nothing about being
number one, but even when we used those,
the kids didn't care. Then we tried doing lots
of other things for them—parties, more
cakes—*and the kids didn't care.* Then it be-
came humiliating to try anymore. So I concentrated on our other team instead. They
didn't win many more games, but, oh, they
appreciated us so much more."

BASIC JUMPS AND VARIATIONS

Split jump

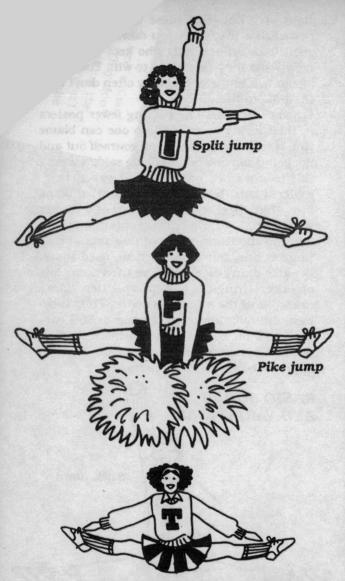

Split jump

Pike jump

Straddle toe-touch jump

78

Stag jump

Bambi

Spread-eagle jump

Tuck

Banana jump

Half "C"

Full "C"

81

Spread-eagle jump

Utah scissors

Utah reach

82

Herky jump

83

Part Five

Squad Captains

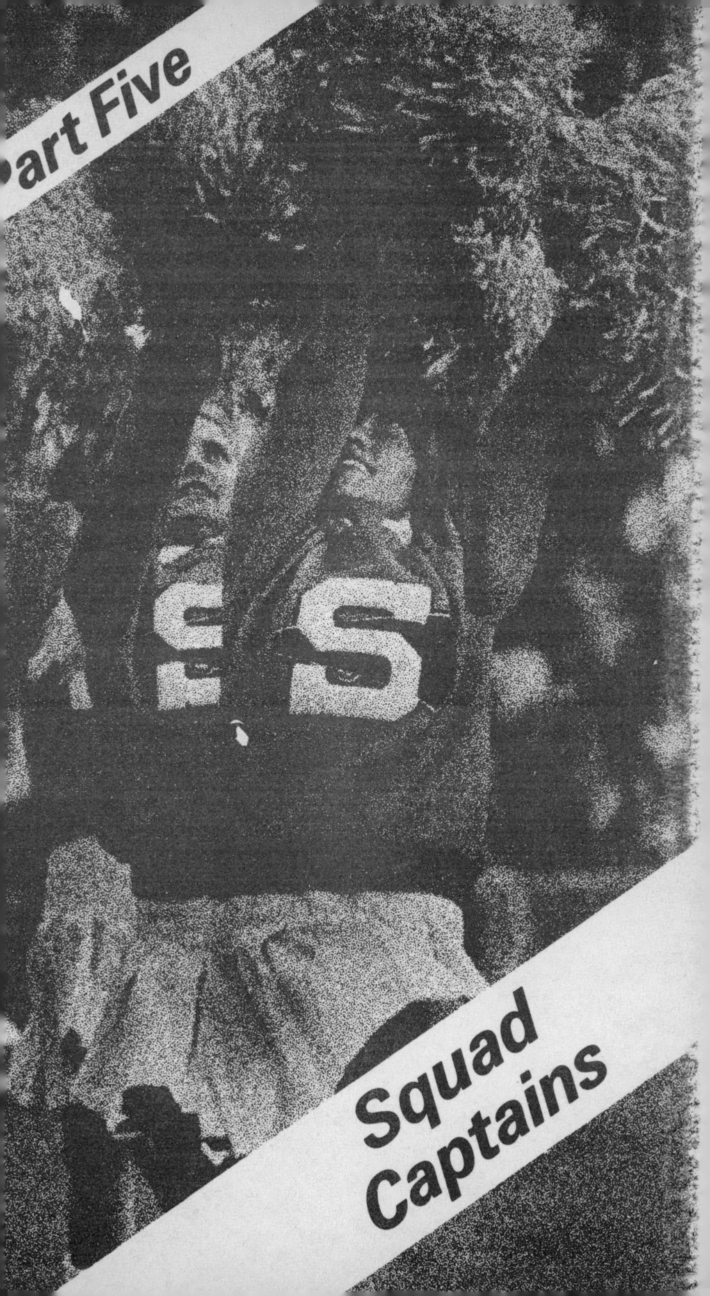

CHAPTER 12

Choosing a Captain

Eventually, senior cheerleaders must say good-bye to the squad and the school.

Before they graduate, however, they usually have one big job ahead of them. They must select a new captain.

Sometimes the cheerleading adviser steps in and does the choosing. But most times, the departing seniors make the big decision.

First, before that decision is made, a big question must be answered: Should we elect one captain, co-captains, or even tri-captains?

Before you wind up with a squad of all chiefs and no Indians, consider the advantages and disadvantages of each situation

"A single captain is best," says Maury, a cheering adviser at a Washington State High School. "It's better for one person to tell friends and peers exactly what to do. It's easier for the squad, too; each cheerleader knows exactly to whom questions should be asked. And there are no questions on who has the authority to run practices and games. Besides, the squad only has to learn the personality of one captain, and the adviser only needs to call on one person for information."

"Having two captains is ideal," rebuts Ed, a cheering adviser for an East Coast private school. "That way, there are two captains to share the responsibilities. It's just too big a job for one person.

"When one captain has a problem, there is another captain there who understands exactly what the other is going through. That helps tremendously. And with *two* people telling their peers what to do, there's usually that much less resistance.

"I've found that two captains can get the work done twice as fast," continues Ed. "Sure, there could be a problem if the two of them don't get along. The squad could take sides and become part of the battle, and I'd wind up spending all my time straightening out the fight. But I've never had that happen. What's always happened is that the two captains choose which duties they'd most like to perform.

"Yes, whenever the senior cheerleaders choose co-captains to head the next year's squad, I breathe a great big sigh of relief."

"It would follow," noted Lucinda, a cheering adviser from a Sun Belt school, "that three captains would be even better than two. Phoning people to give them times, dates, and places is a breeze, because each captain is responsible for making just three phone calls. Each job should become easier because it's shared among three people.

"Yes, it *should* be easier," repeats Lucinda, "but it doesn't work out that way. First comes the differences of opinion among the three; usually, it's two against one, which is never a good situation.

"The squad has a hard time, too, getting used to three personalities. They don't know to whom to turn with a question. Usually, a cheerleader will carefully choose which captain he or she will ask, always picking the one most likely to go along with the cheerleader's own desires. That inevitably leads to a fight when the other two captains hear what the third captain has agreed to.

"Then, if one captain is stronger than the other two, the other two think that he or she is taking over the squad. Then those two band against the third!

"No," Lucinda says, shaking her head, "three captains can be one big headache. No — make that *three* big headaches."

But before you start wondering whether or not you'll be a captain, co-captain, or tri-captain, let's see if you're "captain material" at all.

The Ten Prerequisites for a Good Captain

"When your peers vote you captain," says Kristine, "you know you must be doing a good job."

Earlier in this book, we talked about the ten prerequisites that make up a good cheerleader. It seems that you passed that test. Now here are ten more hurdles to overcome if you're to be the squad's next captain:

1. You must still like cheering. This may seem like a ridiculous point to raise, but some would-be captains have been on the squad so long that they've overdosed on cheers, chants, and mounts. They want to be captains solely because it's an honor they might as well achieve.

Don't try to become captain just because it's the thing to do. It's *not* the thing to do if you're not planning on doing it particularly well.

2. You must be able to work with your cheering adviser and the teams' coaches. Remember: No matter how much support you'll have from your squad on any issue, you'll still have to answer to your adviser. It's your job to function as the adviser's assistant.

If you two have had too many differences of opinion in the past, now's the time to do some patching up. Wipe the slate clean and enjoy your fresh start.

Similarly, you'll have to relate to the teams' coaches and make certain that the cheerleaders perform *exactly* the way the coaches want them to.

3. You must, in spite of new responsibilities, maintain your athletic ability so that you're still able to perform the cheers. It won't do to have a captain who isn't as good as everyone else on the squad for lack of practice time.

4. You must be able to teach others what you've already learned. You'll have to be as patient, uncritical, and generous with time as you possibly can. If there's a kid on the squad whom few like, you'll have to get to know and understand that kid; once the cap-

tain accepts this outsider the rest of the squad will follow suit.

5. You must be organized. A captain can't forget to make brownies if the bake sale is tomorrow. You'll also be accountable for each piece of equipment and all the uniforms. You'll be expected to deal with visiting squads and act as spokesperson. You'll also have to organize incoming seniors on what to do after you've graduated.

6. You must be willing to listen to your squad. Just because you're captain doesn't mean that you have all the answers. Don't abuse your power; if most of the other kids on the squad are telling you that you're wrong about something, they may very well be right. "And if you don't listen to them," notes Arline, "you won't have much of a squad left."

7. You must be proud of your squad. You must believe that your 11 cheerleaders are as good — or *can be* as good — as any squad you've seen.

You may even have to defend them to some people. And if people have a prejudice against cheerleaders, you can imagine what they think of cheerleading *captains*. They perceive them as the biggest idiots in the whole foolish kingdom. It'll be your job to prove them wrong, both on and off the field.

8. You'll have to take the responsibility if the squad does poorly. Like the pitcher in baseball, the quarterback in football, and the goalie in hockey, the captain is charged with the loss if the team doesn't perform up to par.

You'll also have to deal with those cheerleaders who wanted to be captain. And while it's true that most almost-captains are pretty gracious about losing, you can't blame these also-rans for questioning your opinions if they hold different ones. Everyone has tremendous potential to be a Monday morning quarterback; that includes *you*. If you'd lost the race for captain, you'd question the captain's decisions every now and then, too.

9. You must have the respect of your squad. Don't confuse respect with popularity. Perhaps everyone loves you at parties when you come out with a dozen good jokes in a row. But does everyone believe in you and believe that you'd be able to handle a crisis situation?

We've saved the most important for last:

10. You must be able to tell your peers what to do, and you musn't be a tyrant in the process. Can you give orders to *all* the cheerleaders, including those who may have been on the squad longer than you? Can you keep control without becoming too bossy?

The trick in being a leader is being able to *delegate authority to others*. You assign the jobs and then follow up to make certain that everything's proceeding smoothly. In the process, many kids are going to ask you, "Hey, when are *you* going to do something?" You may think it sounds conceited to answer, "The captain oversees the project." But, once again, *they take their cue from you.* Since a captain is the straw that stirs the drink, you shouldn't feel bad about saying that nicely.

As a captain, you'll have your favorites, those kids with whom you see eye to eye. Still, you'll have to make certain that you don't *play* favorites. If you're a really good captain, no one will even know who your favorites are.

Jayne, a cheering adviser who teaches at a Dallas high school, says, "Some years you can turn everything over to a captain, because you know everything will turn out fine. But other years, you can't, because the captain has enough problems just getting to practice on time."

Make sure you're the type of captain who can do it all.

When we gave the ten prerequisites for a good cheerleader, we suggested that you score yes on at least six of those points. Now we're asking for at least *eight* affirmatives if you're to be an effective squad captain.

Part Six

Other Cheerleading Duties

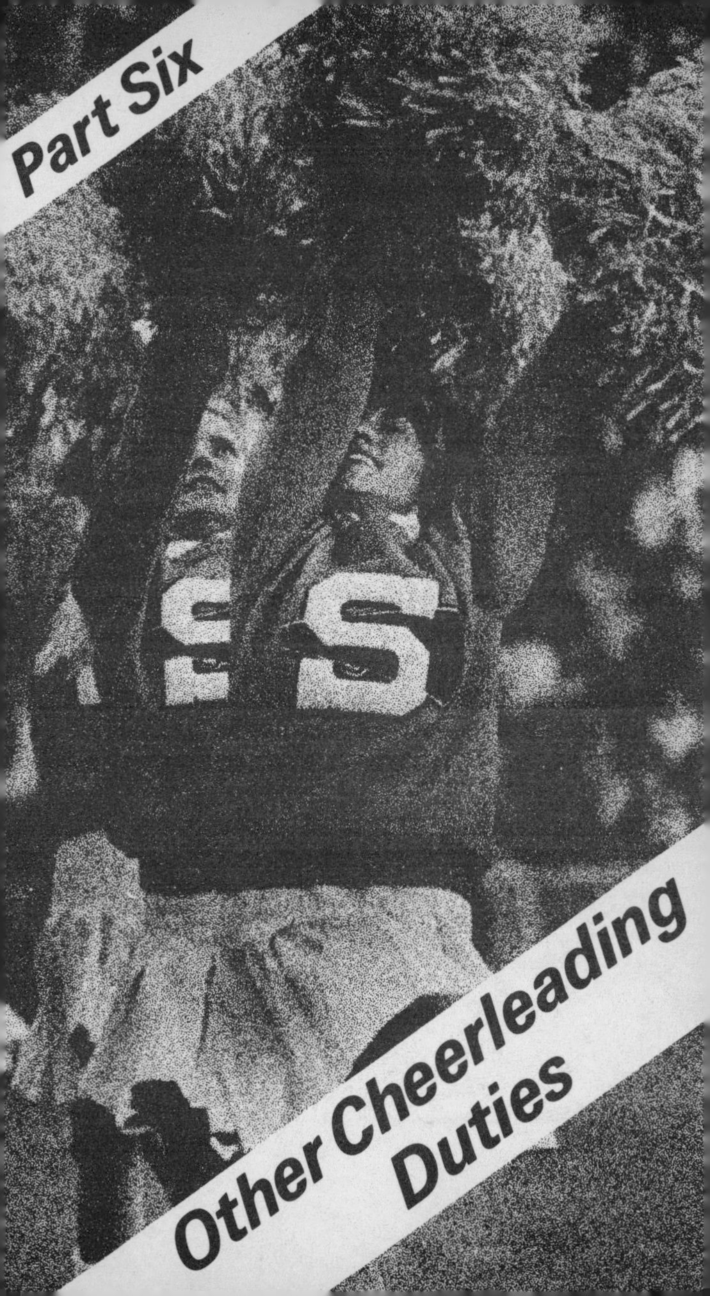

CHAPTER 13

Raising Money

If only your cheerleading duties stopped with practicing and performing! But tradition has had it that cheerleaders are also responsible for a number of other duties, not the least of which is raising money. Sometimes you'll wash cars, because the squad needs new uniforms; sometimes you'll run bake sales, so that you can buy the materials to decorate the gym.

Whatever the reason, you'll find that asking people to part with their hard-earned money in these economic times is going to be very hard work. If there's any consolation here, it's that the practice you'll get raising money as a cheerleader may sharpen your skills for the future, when you're raising funds for a political campaign or a new hospital.

In the meantime, start hawking. Write to a supply house (Cheerleader Supply, Box 30175, Dallas TX 75230, is a good start), get their catalogue, and order what you'll be selling. Keep in mind that you'll sell more moderately priced items than expensive ones. "Don't sell anything that costs more than $3," said Matty, a veteran of three fund-raising campaigns. "Bumper stickers and 'We're Number One!' gloves work best."

A fund raiser that's gaining in popularity is the cheerleading clinic. On a Saturday, arrange to teach third through eighth graders everything they wanted to know about cheerleading but were afraid to ask.

Promote this event in town. Put an ad in the local paper and get them to give you feature coverage as well. Go to the junior high and grammar schools in town — while wearing your uniform — and promote the activity. You probably get out of school before these kids do, so you should be able to make their last-period classes. Always arrange your class visits with the schools' administrators.

Parents will be thrilled to leave their kids for an afternoon, and you'll have a fun time teaching pony mounts to a very receptive audience. "Some kids cried when they had to leave," remembers Ellen.

One last suggestion: Here's a fund raiser that may be the wave of the future.

Many times, various companies will want to do test-marketing surveys in shopping malls: How does this soft drink taste to the average consumer? What does this shopper think of this new breakfast cereal?

Often, agencies love to hand over these duties to groups that will do them for them. And since cheerleaders are bright, energetic types, they're natural salespeople.

A few phone calls to various marketing consultants in your town should put you in touch with the right people.

CHAPTER 14

Pep Rallies

Running a pep rally can take the pep out of you.

It's a pretty exhausting experience. If you were hoping to get a tan this season, you'll be disappointed. Prepare to spend a good deal of time away from the sunlight as you decorate school hallways and locker rooms.

You'll turn into a one-person poster-making factory. It doesn't matter if you have artistic ability or not. Never mind that your last poster was mistaken for a map of Montana — keep creating. So what if you'll go mad trying to think of nicknames, rhymes, and slogans. Somehow, with a little help from your friends, you'll be able to write stuff that might not get you hired as a jingle writer for television commercials but will show your team that you care.

If you're playing a school whose nickname begins with, for example, an *M* (the Miners), get a dictionary and a thesaurus and start plowing through the *M* words so that you can create little epigrams, such as "Maul the Miners." But make certain that when you're choosing slogans you don't choose any that will hurt someone's feelings.

If you can't draw the posters, start gluing. You may feel like you're back in first grade as you cut out pictures from magazines to paste on posters, but you'll come up with some colorful placards.

All in all, it's worth it. This is one time when you won't be competing with a game for the crowd's attention. You're the main attraction.

Of course, that's both good and bad. There will be plenty of tension as time starts ticking away. You'll hear everyone's opinion, and you'll see some tempers flare.

That's because there's plenty of pressure when you're planning your annual pep rally. And, in most schools, there is just one major pep rally per year. True, in some smaller towns, there are monthly pep rallies; a rally serves as entertainment for those outside the school community. But in most schools, a pep rally, like the Academy Awards, the Super Bowl, and Independence Day, occurs only once a year.

So do it right! Pick a time of year when everyone's up for a rally. "The ideal time," says Christine, "is right before the big Thanksgiving Day game."

Get everyone involved. Ask a music teacher to write a song that the cheerleaders can sing. And recruit teachers to be in pep rally skits. You'll find that the younger male teachers may especially be willing to dress up like cheerleaders and appear in a silly skit for the good of the school.

Another nice idea is to invite the parents of the team players, bring them onstage, and introduce them to the crowd. After all, they deserve some of the credit for that MVP quarterback or that game-winning kicker.

A rally should last no longer than 90 minutes. If it's longer it'll have half the impact it would have had if it had been kept at a reasonable length.

But make certain that those 90 minutes are carefully planned. Make sure everyone on the squad knows *precisely* what the order of events is, so you won't hear worrisome cries of "What's next?! What are we doing next?!!" It's also a good idea to have an emergency cheer if something goes wrong. For example, if the band is supposed to play and it looks like it isn't going to start, it's best for you to cover the mistake.

The traditional pep rally has the team walk in as the school song is played. The cheerleaders then give a hello cheer, followed by a cheer for the captain(s) of the team. Then the master of ceremonies is introduced.

Don't wait for the pep rally to discover if you've chosen a good master of ceremonies to lead the show. Consider well in advance who'd be the best person for the job. You might consider the president of the student council, a popular teacher, or, if you're really ambitious, a local hometown celebrity whom everyone knows.

Once the rally is underway, you'll have a chance to teach the spectators the cheers and chants that you'll be using at the big game. Of course, you can showcase everything that you've learned or only give a sneak preview of what you plan to do on game day.

You'll have to have a policeman on hand for a pep rally; it's the law. Happily, the police enjoy working with cheerleaders, because they're "a nice group of kids." They'll be supportive of what you're doing, and it will be an education for you, too.

Mascots

Should you adopt a mascot?

Some squads like to take a furry little animal, dress him in some sort of uniform, and parade him on the field. But tending to an animal and its needs is often a difficult, and occasionally messy, task.

As a result, some squads use a young kid as a mascot. They'll dress a ten-year-old as an Indian (or whatever represents their team) and let him romp around, projecting even more pep and joy than his elders.

But using a young kid leads to problems, too. Who's going to take care of him? Who's going to fetch him a Coke when he complains he's thirsty?

The best mascot? The would-be cheerleader who *just* missed making the squad. Dress him or her as a representative of the team's nickname, or go all the way and create your own San Diego Chicken. Such a mascot is sure to get the crowd going.

One last word: Work hand-in-hand with the mascot to make certain that nobody upstages anyone else.

Part Seven

Cheering Camps

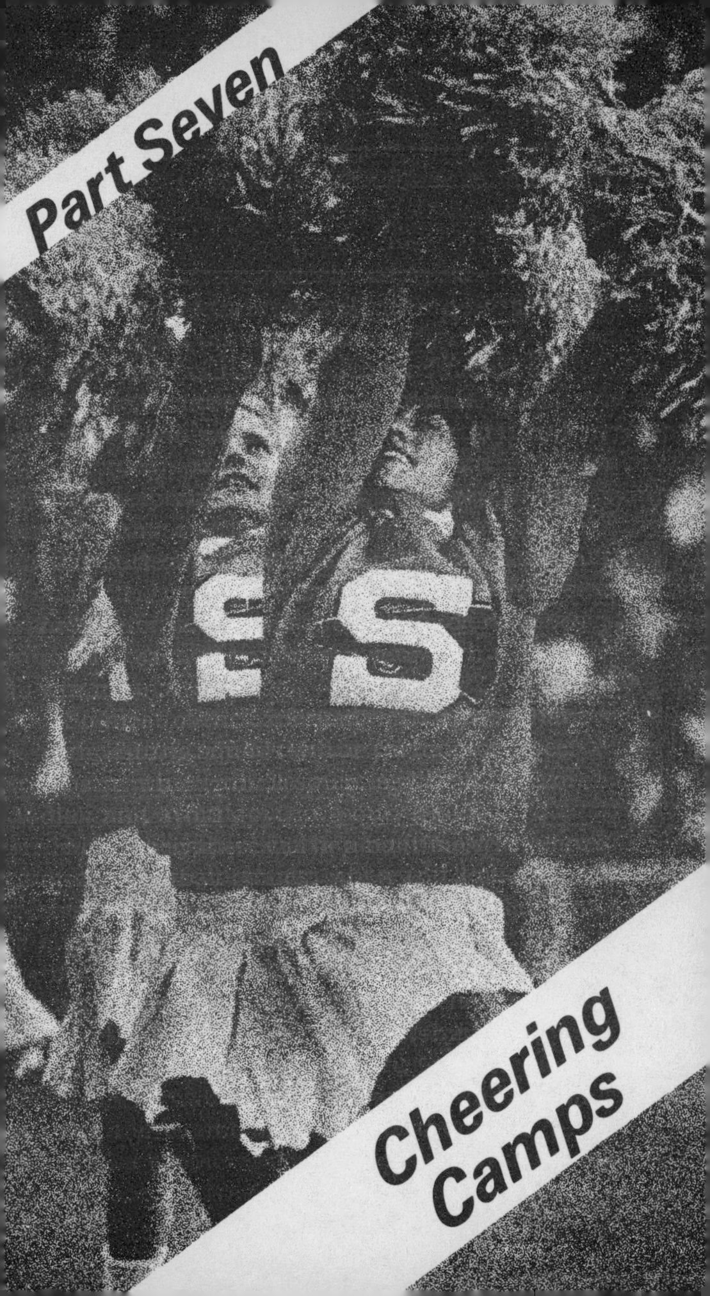

C H A P T E R 15

Going to a Cheering Camp

If you want your cheers to be snappier and your stunts to be more daring, consider a visit to a cheerleading camp.

At camp, you'll have a chance to perform for other squads and judges. You'll learn quite a bit from both.

Camp is where you perfect what you'll be performing in the upcoming year. It would seem to be a place where you'd work harder than ever before.

Not necessarily. It's hard to work when you're in a rustic setting of forests and live deer. Practice won't seem as real as it does on the floor of the gym. Perhaps you'll convulse with laughter at your third unsuccessful attempt to do a pyramid. Flying arms and bent wrists won't seem all that terrible.

But — the movements and voices of every cheerleader on the squad must be perfectly synchronized even in camp. Not that the spirit and fun of cheering camp won't shine through; of course it will. In fact, if it doesn't, you've got a problem. If it looks like you're struggling, the audience is going to get tired before you do.

One of the best aspects of camp is getting away from it all. It's always fun to be on your own and see someplace new. And when a hundred or so cheerleaders get together, there are bound to be adventures.

"Our most outrageous episode occurred not at camp," says Leslie, "but at the airport. As we waited for our plane to be serviced, we practiced yells, cheers, and mounts. People didn't know what to make of us; some passers-by took pictures of us; some seemed frightened. And when we spotted Glen Campbell waiting for *his* plane, we serenaded him with a medley of his own songs."

That's a nice change from sitting around the house on some hot August afternoon.

Actually, cheering camps, which traditionally were held in late August (a logical time to have a crash course in cheering — just before the school year) now seem to favor June. "The feeling is," explains Alma, an adviser of two championship squads, "that you should start the summer knowing what you need to learn by the time school starts. Why wait till the first of September to discover you need pyramid work, when you can discover it by July first and work on it all summer?"

One of the major conflicts of cheering camp will be whether to practice during free hours or not.

It's a tough decision to make. If you've spent the entire morning almost getting everything down pat, should you spend the free time perfecting routines or water-skiing?

"Water-skiing," insists Lee. "When's the next time you're going to have a lake, boats, and skis right under your nose? Besides, all work and no play makes John a dull boy."

"Practice," suggests Dale. "That's what you're there for."

How about a compromise? Take the total number of hours the camp is available for both *practice time* and *free time*. If you allot two-thirds (or a little less) of the time to practice, you'll never have to worry that you didn't practice enough.

But practice does, as they say, make perfect. In the words of Leslie, "When it happened, when it all came together after the long hours of practice, everyone knew it. It was like magic. You could feel it flow with the other kids, and you could see it in the eyes of the people watching. We knew we had it."

Get a group of cheerleaders together, and they can't stop cheering, no matter where they are. As a result, be prepared for some informal cheerleading practice at dinnertime.

There always seems to be someone who thinks it's a good idea to show the other squads what his squad accomplished that day. "I always plan to rest my voice at dinnertime," reports Ellen, "but there is something to be said for repeating and relearning the cheers without pressure. Nobody has to worry about making a mistake. In fact, here's the time to make mistakes. Now that you've made that one particular wrong move, you probably won't make it during the competition."

And there are plenty of opportunities to make mistakes in competitions: Cheerleading camps hold one competition each night. So, not long after you've stuffed yourself with every piece of food you can find, you'll have to stuff yourself into a uniform and compete.

This is where the hard work pays off. Do a good job so that tomorrow you'll enjoy the water-skiing you missed while practicing today.

There are myths and rumors concerning in which position you should perform in a competition program. "If you go first," says Jean, "you'll set the tone and give everyone a hard act to follow." Alan disagrees: "Perform first, and they'll forget you by the time the fourth squad goes on."

"Last is best," claims Ronnie. "Do a good job, and the judges won't be able to remember anything that's happened before." Joanie counters with, "Last is the worst. All the other cheerleaders are loose because they've already performed, the pressure is off. Now they just want to laugh and jeer whenever you do something wrong."

And so the arguments go. For the record, most of the judges we talked to said the same thing: They've been to plenty of cheering camps, they've judged many times, and they know how to pick the winning squad regardless of position.

After the nightly competition is over, all the squads, be they winners or losers, get along pretty well. After all, when you're only kings and queens for a night, everyone can afford to be gracious. Tomorrow, every squad will get another chance to win the blue ribbons.

Togetherness is wonderful and all that, but after a while, you'll discover everyone's flaws, both in cheerleading and in personality. Communal living can be difficult. Consider how much smoother your own family runs when there's even one fewer person (and opinion) around the house.

So you are bound to get on some cheerleader's nerves, perhaps before someone gets on yours. Chuck's whistling, Fran's knuckle-cracking, and Lee's playing with food may have seemed funny on day one, but they don't seem as endearing on day three.

Admit it: You might even get a little homesick. Perhaps one of your friends inadvertently scheduled a party for a night that you're away. "I missed being at home for my birthday," says Kristine wistfully.

Some kids cope better than others. If you're not doing so well, count up the number of hours until you leave camp. No matter how high the number is, it always decreases.

Still, cheering camp is the ideal way to build a foundation for the rest of the year. At first, you'll find the strengths and weaknesses of your fellow cheerleaders; eventually, you'll learn how each of them contributes different values to the squad.

Probably the only thing better than going to cheering camp is returning the following year. When you see the cabin once again, you'll remember how those private jokes and nicknames got started. The whole place will be the sight for sore eyes that you hear older people talk about.

That's why we recommend taking your camera when you go to camp. Remember to take plenty of film, too, so you won't have to pay the high prices of the local stores. On the other hand, if you *do* forget to take film from home, buy it, anyway. You'll never be able to get shots like this again.

Cheering Camp Evaluations

Each day you're at cheering camp, you'll be judged in certain categories. Below is a typical checklist that is given to each judge. This should help you to know what the professionals are looking for:

ENTRANCE AND EXIT
  a. spirit
  b. skill
  c. audience appeal

CHEER EXECUTION
  a. motions
  b. creativity and originality
  c. International Cheerleading
     Foundation cheer
  d. home cheer

CHEERING SKILLS
  a. jumps
     1. execution
     2. variety
     3. effective use
  b. gymnastics
     1. execution
     2. effective use
  c. partner stunts
     1. execution
     2. effective use

    d. pyramids
      1. execution
      2. effective use

GENERAL PERFORMANCE
    a. personality projection
    b. squad unity
    c. eye contact
    d. voice
    e. appearance
    f. poise and confidence
    g. effort and improvement
    h. overall effectiveness

ONE FINAL WORD

cheerleader 'chi(ə)r-,led-ər *n*: one that calls
for and directs organized cheering.

Well, that's how the most recent *Webster's New Collegiate Dictionary* defines the word. You'll find it on page 190, right between "cheerio" and "cheerless."

But we hope you know now that being a cheerleader has more to it than the dictionary definition gives it credit for. If *we* had a crack at that dictionary, we'd describe a cheerleader as a happy, healthy individual. That's because 92% of the former cheerleaders we interviewed said they'd try out for the squad again if they had the chance, and 97% said that they felt the training and exercise they got while cheering was definitely worthwhile.

Most of those cheerleaders were *A* students, too. But as we said earlier, cheering is its own reward.

Game schedules

Write your own cheers

Write your own cheers

Squad formations

Squad formations

Squad members'
phone numbers

Special activities

Reminders